SO-CFN-590

GOODBYE TO CAMP CRUMB

by

Jerry J. Mallett and Marian R. Bartch

A Tumtwit Series book

A Perma-Bound Book

Hertzberg-New Method, Inc.   Jacksonville, Illinois

GOODBYE TO CAMP CRUMB

BOOKS BY MARIAN R. BARTCH
AND JERRY J. MALLETT

Good Old Ernie

Poor Old Ernie

*The First and Last Gravelsburg Elementary
    School Spelling Bee*

A Bellyful of Ballet

Close the Curtains

On Your Mark...Get Set...HELP!

Goodbye to Camp Crumb

For Judy Butler,
a special friend.

ABOUT THE AUTHORS

Jerry J. Mallett and Marian R. Bartch both teach in the Education Division at Findlay College in Ohio. Together they have written the *Ernie* series (Perma Bound), and the *Tumtwit* series (Perma Bound), fiction for children. Books for teachers and librarians include *Reading Rousers* (Goodyear), *Stories to Draw* (Freline), *Elementary Library Resource Kit* (Center for Applied Research in Education), and *Math Motivators* (Goodyear).

It is the expressed hope of the authors that their works will help motivate children to read as well as aiding them in the development of a sense of humor.

Dr. Mallett received his B.S. degree from Ohio University, his Master of Education and doctorate from the University of Toledo. Dr. Bartch has a B.S. degree from Findlay College, Master of Education from Bowling Green State University, and her doctorate from the University of Toledo.

ABOUT THE ILLUSTRATOR

Mark D. Smith has fifteen years experience as a professional artist and illustrator. He has been an art educator for twelve years at the secondary level with the Findlay City Schools. Mr. Smith received his B.A. degree from Bowling Green State University.

A DIVISION OF HERTZBERG NEW METHOD, INC.
VANDALIA ROAD • JACKSONVILLE, IL. 62650

Chapter One

"Please fill in the first two rows," said Mrs. Tumtwit as our fourth-grade class filed into the auditorium.

"Tweeeeeeet!" sounded a shrill whistle.

"Here comes the Bull with her whistle," whispered Henry Dukes, my very best friend.

"Yeah," I whispered back. "We sure are lucky we didn't get her as our teacher this year."

Mrs. Bullbarg was the other fourth-grade teacher at the Gravelsburg Elementary School. Years ago, the kids had nicknamed her the Bull. The name stuck because it really described her so well. She is as wide as she is tall and, on a good day, is about as pleasant as a mean bull. And she never goes anywhere in the school without her whistle.

Two more of those whistle blasts and fifty-two fourth-graders were seated in the proper rows.

Mr. Duddle, our principal, was standing in front of us.

"Boys and girls," he shouted to get our attention.

"TWEEEEEEET!"

"Thank you, Mrs. Bullbarg," said Mr. Duddle. He

really didn't look like he was very thankful for her help, though.

"Boys and girls," he began again. He waited a moment as if expecting another whistle blast. When none came, he went on.

"As you already know, you fourth-graders are in for a big treat. You will soon be off on a great learning adventure. This has all been made possible for you through Mrs. Tumtwit's hard work and the financial help of the P.T.A. Yes, boys and girls, soon each and every one of you will have the opportunity to dip into that great well of knowledge...nature! Tomorrow you will begin your over-night outdoor education experiment. And, I might add, if this goes as well as I am certain it will," he smiled and nodded in Mrs. Tumtwit's direction as he spoke, "this will become an *annual* event at the Gravelsburg Elementary School. Just think of that! An annual event!"

He beamed at all of us, then went on. "Now I asked for this meeting to go over some last minute details. Let me first remind you of those items you are to take. They are listed on the letter Mrs. Tumtwit wrote to your parents. Please be sure to bring *all* of those items to school with you tomorrow morning. We will be leaving for Camp Crumb at eight o-clock sharp." He stopped and looked blankly at Mrs. Tumtwit. "Wasn't there something else I needed to say?" She waved a stack of permission slips.

"Oh, yes," he said. "Two students *still* have not brought in their permissions slips. If you two don't bring them in tomorrow, you will *not* be allowed to go to camp! This is very important...do not forget!"

I looked at Henry and pointed. He shook his head no and shrugged his shoulders.

"The two students are...Bernice Batsdaffy...and, and..."

"Well, of course, who else?" I thought to myself. "Naturally it would be Bernice, the dumbest kid in our school. Well, if not the dumbest, certainly the biggest pain." Everyone turned to look at her. I couldn't believe it. She just sat there in the second row beaming as if she'd been given an award or something.

"And I can't seem to remember..." groped Mr. Duddle. Mrs. Tumtwit jumped out of her seat and handed him a slip of paper.

"Oh, yes...the other student is Lawrence Lopp. Lawrence, we need your permission slip."

"I brung it in already," declared Lawrence, jumping up. Mr. Duddle cringed visibly, then said, "No, Lawrence, you *brought* it in."

"Yeah...that's just what I said, Mr. Duddle, I already brung it in!" agreed Lawrence.

"Lawrence...I believe you're confused," said our principal. Boy, was that ever an understatement! Lawrence confused? He was about on the same level as Bernice. This was his second year in fourth-grade and he thought he just automatically knew more than any other kid...or teacher, for that matter...in grade four.

"I know I brung it in!" Lawrence was beginning to get defensive.

"When did you brun...uh, bring it in?" questioned Mrs. Tumtwit, turning in her seat to look at him.

"Last week. My ma signed it and everything. My

4

dad give me a lickin'!"

"Oh, Lawrence," sighed our teacher, turning back to look at Mr. Duddle again. "*That* was your report card."

I heard some snickers from the other kids and saw Joe punch Tom and say something. Joe Santora and Tom Toevich are two of my best friends...next to Henry, that is. The four of us had really been looking forward to our overnight campout...or, as Mr. Duddle calls it..."our great learning adventure." We were all excited about going to Camp Crumb and hoped to get to bunk in the same cabin.

"And now," continued Mr. Duddle, "let me tell you that four adults will be going along for your educational benefits and, of course, supervision. Mrs. Tumtwit..."

Our class yelled and clapped at the mention of her name. I could see that her face was getting red. Mr. Duddle went on, "...yes, we're all pleased. Mrs. Tumtwit will be the camp director for she has been responsible for the organization of the entire project. Mr. Lowpitch..." Another round of clapping and yelling went on, this time from both classes. Mr. Lowpitch is our music teacher and everyone really likes him a lot.

"Mr. Lowpitch will be in charge of your field arts class and the evening camp fire program. As some of you already know, Mrs. Bullbarg..." Mr. Duddle waited here for applause. When there was none, he continued. "...will not be able to participate in our outdoor education program, due to her allergies."

I whispered to Henry, "Too bad she isn't allergic to metal whistles."

"Ms. Strider will go in her place..." Mr. Duddle was

interrupted by approving applause. Ms. Strider is our health/gym teacher who sometimes gets carried away with the idea of physical fitness, but we all like her anyway.

"Ms. Strider will wear many hats while at Camp Crumb. She will be nurse, lifeguard, *and* be in charge of the fitness activities. I just want to say here, boys and girls, that I hope you will all be careful enough so that no one will need her services as a lifeguard." He paused and looked around at us. "That just leaves one more person," he said, with his eyes twinkling. "That person is yours truly, Dillingham D. Duddle."

He paused again, waiting. There was a smattering of applause, led by our teachers. "I will assume the role of nature expert. You see, boys and girls, my undergraduate degree was in nature interpretation and I..."

As Mr. Duddle droned on about his qualifications, Joe and Tom looked back at me. Joe crossed his eyes, Tom made a face like he was gagging. I nudged Henry and we both made faces back at them.

"Now then...I've asked Loretta Livermost to tell us a little about Camp Crumb. As you know, Loretta is new to our school this year. What you might not know is that her father used to be the director of Camp Crumb before moving to Gravelsburg. Loretta?"

Loretta was sitting next to her best friend, Roberta Roundly. I noticed she gave her a worried look as she got out of her seat. As she walked to the front of the auditorium I heard Joe begin to sing-song, "Woo...woo...woo...and Bobby too!"

"Here we go again," I thought to myself. Ever since Loretta and I were the co-chairpersons of our school-wide spelling bee last fall, the guys never miss a chance to tease me about her. Actually I think they are just jealous because Loretta is clearly the prettiest girl in our class... maybe the entire school...and she shows that she likes me.

"Camp Crumb is about seventy miles from Gravelsburg," she began.

"Boy," I thought, "you sure got to hand it to her. I know I sure would hate to get up in front of everybody like that."

"There are four cabins. Two for girls, and two for boys. They are built on a hill. The girls' cabins are near the top and the boys' near the bottom. In between is the camp circle, mess hall, and activity field. This is about the only flat piece of land in the camp. Below the boys' cabins you'll find the lake and the beach. You can swim and boat in the lake. That's all."

Loretta was about to hurry back to her seat when Mr. Duddle stopped her by saying, "Very good, Loretta. Do any of you have any questions to ask Loretta before she sits down? Yes, Joe?"

"What kind of boats are they?"

"Rowboats and canoes," answered Loretta. "And, oh yes, something new...sail surfers."

"Sail surfers...what are they?" Joe asked.

"Well," said Loretta, "They're kind of hard to describe. But they look like surf boards with sails attached. They're hard to manage though."

Mr. Duddle laughed and said, "Yes, some people find them hard to manage, but they don't have the experience with sailing craft that your principal and nature expert has. If you just watch how I do it, you'll see how really

8

easy it is to sail them. Now, any other questions... comments? Yes, Lawrence?"

"Why don't they clean up the mess?"

Loretta looked at Mr. Duddle with a puzzled expression.

"What do you mean?" asked Mr. Duddle.

"That mess she said was on the flat spot."

Mrs.Tumtwit broke in with, "I think Lawrence is referring to the mess hall."

"Yeah...for sure...that's it," said Lawrence.

"No...no...no...you don't understand, Lawrence," explained our principal. "You see, the mess hall is the building in which you eat all your meals. 'Mess' is just the name it's called. Yes, Bernice, what's your question?"

"Where do you go to the bathroom?"

"Leave it to Bernice to ask that question," Henry whispered.

Loretta's face turned red as she answered, "There are two latrines. One for boys and one for girls."

Somehow the term "latrine" struck Lawrence as funny.

"Ho, ho, ho...latrine...ha, ha, har!" he guffawed.

"TWEEEEEEET!" blared the whistle.

"Alright now. Thank you, Loretta," Mr. Duddle said quickly. "Now, let me remind you once again...don't forget to bring your supplies with you to school tomorrow *and* be sure to get a good night's sleep. You'll want to be fresh-as-a-daisy for your great learning adventure." We were then dismissed to go back to our rooms.

Chapter Two

Our bus rolled through the entrance to Camp Crumb at mid-morning. Before the driver opened the door, Mrs. Tumtwit stood up in front. "Now, group, what are you going to do first? Who remembers?" As if one, all voices shouted, "Find our cabins!" "And..." prompted our teacher. "Make up our bunks."

Tom, Joe, Henry, and I were really pleased that we had been assigned to the same cabin.

"Now what do you suppose this 'nature walk' thing is?" asked Tom. He had made up his bunk in record time and was sitting on it watching the rest of us struggle with ours.

"I guess we'll probably walk through the woods or something like that," Joe answered, shoving his sheet under the mattress.

"Oh great," Henry chimed in. "Old Dilly Duddle will show us the difference between a squirrel and a rabbit."

"Yeah," I laughed, putting the final touches on my bunk. "I've always gotten those two mixed up."

11

"Oh, I know the difference between them," Tom said. "I do have trouble though, telling the difference between a squirrel and a Batsdaffy!"

We were all just standing around laughing at our own cleverness after finishing our bunks when the camp bell rang. This was the signal, we had been told, to drop whatever we were doing to hurry to the camp's meeting circle.

• • • • •

"You are to stay together at all times," droned Mr. Duddle. "No one, and I mean absolutely *no one*, is to go off alone! Is that understood?"

We nodded our heads in agreement with a chorus of yeses and uhus. Mr. Duddle must have been nearing the end of his rules for our nature walk. It seemed to me that he had been going on for hours already. We were all sitting in the camp circle anxious to get started *doing* something. He was standing on a large rock to talk to us. There was a huge pair of binoculars dangling from his neck and he had changed into hiking shorts.

"Mr. Duddle...Mr. Duddle!"

"Yes, Bernice?"

"Mr. Duddle...I brought my notebook and pencils."

"That's nice, Bernice."

I was hardly surprised because Bernice never goes *anywhere* without her precious notebook and an astounding supply of freshly sharpened pencils.

"How do you suppose she'll sharpen those marvelous pencils way out in the woods?" Henry quietly asked me. His question was soon answered when Bernice went on.

13

"Mr. Duddle...Mr. Duddle!"

"Yes, Bernice. What *is* it now?"

"My daddy bought me a Daffy Duck pencil sharpener to bring along with me to camp." She proceeded to demonstrate by sharpening an already fine-point pencil.

I noticed Loretta and Roberta exchange looks of pure exasperation. Mr. Duddle glanced at Mrs. Tumtwit and sighed. Then he continued. "Now we must begin our nature walk by keeping our eyes open. I want everyone to keep their eyes and ears alert to the new surroundings. One never knows when one will come upon some unusually rich find."

"GOLD? Would they be *GOLD* mines?" asked Lawrence. His face brightened for the first time since Mr. Duddle began his speech.

"Gold what, Lawrence?" asked our puzzled principal.

"Gold...the mines. You just said we might come across a rich mine."

"No...no! Not a mine, Lawrence. A FIND! I said we might FIND something really exciting or interesting. I did *not* mention a *mine!*" We could tell that Mr. Duddle was more than a little annoyed with Lawrence's interruption.

"Now where was I?" he continued. "Oh, yes. We will all go off into the great wilderness to rediscover nature. Who knows what stimulating knowledge awaits us."

I heard a low "Yuk!" from Joe.

"I want you to keep your eyes open...I want you to keep your ears open," our principal repeated, pointing to his eyes and ears as if he were doing finger plays with the kindergartners. He was gesturing more and more wildly as he spoke.

"Make sure you look...look...look! Look under the rocks. Look around the bushes. Look high up in the trees. Look into the..."

"LOOK OUT!" yelled Mrs. Tumtwit. It was too late.

"Yeow!" hollered Mr. Duddle as he "looked" himself right off the rock and fell to the ground with a loud thud!

• • • • •

"How much longer do you think this nature walk is going to last?" asked Joe.

"Not much longer, I hope," groaned Henry.

"I think six hours is more than long enough," I said. "We are sure over that now."

"Yeah, more like eight hours," added Tom.

Loretta looked at us and sympathized, "It's only been about an hour, but it sure does seem a lot longer."

"If I have to look at one more Yellow Breasted Sap Sucker I'm going to throw up!" complained Henry.

"Just keep moving. We must be near the end," I told them.

"My feet hurt!" moaned Roberta.

"So do..."

Loretta's comment was cut short by a loud, excited yell from Mr. Duddle. "Oh, look...look right down there!"

Our leader had stopped our merry band of nature lovers at the edge of a small ravine. He was pointing to the bottom of it and practically jumping up and down in his excitement. "Oh, boys and girls! How wonderful, wonderful, FERNS! FERNS! I was just hoping we'd be fortunate enough to have the treat of seeing these rare and

ancient beauties!"

"Mr. Duddle...Mr. Duddle...how do you spell ferns?" asked Bernice. She was writing down the name of every living and non-living thing that we'd happened upon, in her stupid notebook.

"F-E-R-N," spelled Mr. Duddle.

"Boy, now isn't that a really hard word to spell!" commented Henry.

"Yeah," I agreed, "and to think she won the school-wide spelling bee last fall!"

"FERNS, boys and girls. These magnificent plants grew as tall as trees during prehistoric times," enthused our guide and nature expert.

"I think we've been on this walk *since* prehistoric times!" Tom complained.

We all agreed with him.

"Boys and girls, I hope you can appreciate..." Mr. Duddle froze in mid-sentence. He didn't move a muscle. He didn't say a word. He didn't even seem to breathe. He looked ready to burst. I began to wonder if he was having some kind of attack.

"Oh, no...it can't be...it just can't be!" He was quiet for a moment as if listening, then said, "It is! Oh, it is! Boys and girls...I can't believe our luck. Now listen carefully...very carefully."

It became deathly quiet. I looked at Henry and he just rolled up his eyes.

"I suppose it's another Yellow Breasted Sap Sucker," he whispered disgustedly.

Mr. Duddle drew in a sharp breath and asked in a loud whisper, "Hear that? Do you all hear that?"

We all bobbed our heads up and down hoping that would end the matter. I figured that not even *one* weary hiker had heard whatever it was that Mr. Duddle was so taken with. The only sounds I could hear were Lawrence swatting at a mosquito and the scraping of the Daffy Duck pencil sharpener.

"It's coming from the Pin Oak," our nature-lover leader told us in hushed tones. He was pointing to a tree at the bottom of the ravine.

"Be quiet, and follow me. But be very quiet," He began to lower himself down the side of the ravine.

Joe turned around and said quietly, "What you bet it's a Dark-Hatched Dippidy-Dilly-Duddle?"

"Yeah," Tom agreed. We all tried not to laugh out loud at that. Actually it took all of our concentration just to keep our balance on the steep slope as we were going down. We were slipping and sliding, for the side was not only steep, it was also damp.

"There...again...hear it?" asked our principal in a loud stage whisper.

I was grasping a sapling to try to stop my uncontrollable descent. Loretta slid into my back.

"Oh, I'm sorry, Bob." she said.

"Here," I said, "grab a hold of this tree." I could see that Henry had two hands full of weeds and his feet braced on a rock. Others were clinging precariously to the side of the steep ravine any way they could. Mr. Duddle was totally unaware of our difficulties, intent only on the "sound."

"Boys and girls, you are about to see...to see one of the rarest sights in our state."

18

"Yeah," interjected Tom, just loud enough for us guys to hear. "Bernice will go out of her cabin without her notepad and pencils."

"You are about to see..." repeated Mr. Duddle, his excitement growing with every word, "you are about to see...a Gravel Gray Grunt!"

Well, I do know he went on talking and talking about this wonderful, thrilling FIND, but his words were totally lost on those of us trying to cling to the ravine wall. We were all too busy attempting to keep from laughing at him *and* plunging to our deaths below to hear anything more. There were some coughs and throat clearing to cover up the laughs. I did hear Lawrence let go with a couple of snorts from his place somewhere near the top of the ravine.

"Mr. Duddle...Mr. Duddle," whined Bernice.

"G-R-U-N-T." spelled Mr. Duddle. Then he turned to face the cliff-hangers and said sternly, "You will *have* to be quiet from this point on! I don't want any of you to do anything to scare off that rare little fellow."

Bernice Batsdaffy was close to his heels. She was carrying her notebook and pencil in her mouth for she needed both hands to continue the death-defying descent.

"Oh...watch out," whispered Tom.

"Your foot is digging in my back," complained Henry as quietly as he could.

"I can't help it," mouthed Joe.

"Oh...I think I've torn a hole in my jeans," whispered Roberta.

"Oooofff!" I groaned as I slid into a big jagged rock.

"I think I just broke my arm," someone else whispered.

Mr. Duddle was about half way down into the ravine, clinging to a bush with one hand. He turned and placed his finger on his lips. Then he held his binoculars to his eyes, scanning the Pin Oak. Next, he gave a "forward-ho" signal like the wagon masters in old western movies. The hikers slid onward.

"I think it's getting steeper," I whispered to Henry.

"Yeah. I'm not sure the Gravel Gray Grunt is worth this."

"I *know* the Gravel Gray Grunt isn't worth this!"

Just then, Mr. Duddle stopped dead in his tracks his binoculars still focused on the big tree. His arm raised in the halt position. Now it wasn't that we didn't try to follow his command. We really did. But we must have built up so much momentum coming down the slope that we just couldn't "halt." I mean, we couldn't even come close to a "halt." Actually, a few of the kids who were near rocks or bushes did manage to slow down a little. But it was no use...it didn't help. Kids began sliding and falling into one another just like a stack of dominoes knocking each other over. In less than a few seconds, the ravine was alive with screams, yells, shouts, and groans. Mr. Duddle plunged into the ravine as fifty-two fourth-graders steamrollered over him.

It took some time to untangle ourselves and find out that no one was hurt. Mr. Duddle was the last one to get up. He stood there a few minutes staring at the broken binoculars in his hand. He seemed a bit dazed. Then, without looking directly at any of us, he said in a somewhat subdued voice, "I hope you have all learned

something on our nature walk." We were then led straight back to our cabins. Mr. Duddle walked along in complete silence all the way.

23

Chapter Three

Our tattered and torn band of nature lovers returned to camp just in time for lunch. We were directed to the latrines by Mrs. Tumtwit who told us that we had to clean up before we entered the mess hall.

The guys and I ate at a table with Mr. Lowpitch. We described all that had taken place on our nature walk to him. He could hardly eat for laughing so much. We kept looking around the mess hall for Mr. Duddle, but he never showed up. We found out later that he had gone to his cabin to lie down and rest. I guess the excitement of discovering a Gravel Gray Grunt was simply too much for him.

After lunch we divided into three groups. Mrs. Tumtwit, Ms. Strider, and Mr. Lowpitch each took a group and taught us a different subject. We rotated from one teacher to another and were taught field-math, field-science, and field-arts. It was all pretty relaxed and a lot of fun.

"Too bad school can't be like this all the time," said Henry as we left field-science and walked to Mr. Lowpitch for field-arts.

"Yeah," I agreed. "This sure beats sitting around in a

dumb old classroom any day."

"You know what I really miss though? Oh, I *really* do miss it!" said Joe.

"No...what?" asked Henry.

"The Bull's whistle!"

We all laughed as Henry cuffed Joe on the shoulder.

Even though the classes were different and fun, we were only too glad when they ended. The reason was simple. We were going to get to go swimming next. We raced back to our cabins to change.

"I *know* my bathing suit is in here somewhere...but where?" said Henry, rummaging through his suitcase.

"Boy, I put mine right on top," said Joe, starting to undress.

"Oh, here it is," Henry said in a relieved voice.

I poked Henry and said, "Look at Lawrence."

Lawrence was stepping into the biggest pair of boxer bathing trunks I had ever seen. Joe and Tom had noticed them too.

"Hey, Lawrence," hollered Tom. "Where'd you get that bathing suit?"

"It's my oldest brother's," he hollered back. "What's it to you?"

"What is your older brother...a gorilla?" teased Tom.

"Yeah," added Joe. "His name is King Kong!"

Now Tom and Joe should have known better than to start anything with Lawrence. Everybody in Gravelsburg knew how mean the whole Lopp clan is. Not only that, but since this was Lawrence's *second* year in fourth-grade, he was a good head taller than any other boy in the class... and a lot heavier.

"You better take that back!" yelled Lawrence.

"Hey...we were only kidding," Tom said, as his face turned pale.

"Yeah," said Joe. "Can't you take a joke?"

"You're gonna be sorry!" yelled Lawrence as he tripped on King Kong's bathing trunks. Before he had them all the way up and tied, he was running in our direction. Tom and Joe left a trail of clothes behind them as they raced out of the cabin pulling up their swim suits.

● ● ● ● ●

"Hurry up...hurry up..." boomed Ms. Strider as we came down the hill toward the beach. She already had those who were there lined up in rows.

"Oh, oh...calisthenics time," I groaned.

"Oh, gosh," moaned Henry. "why can't we just go for a swim?"

We joined the formation. I noticed that Tom and Joe had found safe places right in front of Ms. Strider. Lawrence was down a couple of rows from them. He kept glaring at them.

"Hurry up, girls. We're all waiting for you," yelled Ms. Strider. About a dozen girls came down the hill. They seemed to be a bit shy about getting down to the rest of us. Probably had something to do with their bathing suits. Loretta and Roberta were already in the line-up.

"Ms. Strider...Ms. Strider."

"Yes, Bernice? What is it?"

"Will you take a picture of me doing my calisthenics?"

"No, Bernice, I will not."

"But Ms. Strider, my daddy bought me this Wacko Instant Double-Charge Camera just so I could bring it to camp," pleaded Bernice, holding her new camera up for everyone to see. "Please, Ms. Strider."

"No, Bernice."

"But my daddy wants..."

"Bernice! Enough! I will not take a picture of you doing calisthenics. When we are finished, I *will* take your picture in the water or on the beach. Now put the camera down somewhere so we can get started!"

Bernice was all smiles. She took the camera over to a large piece of driftwood and set it down.

"Okay, everybody...let's go! It's jumping-jacks time! One, two, one, two, one, two...STOP! Lawrence...please stay in your place and stop moving up a row."

Tom and Joe looked nervously over their shoulders. I could see Lawrence mouth, "You're dead!" in their direction. Well, jumping-jacks turned into touch-your-toes which became deep-knee bends which changed into jogging-in-place which led to push-ups that finally evolved into sit-ups.

It was during sit-ups that I noticed Lawrence scooting up his row with each sit-up he did. Sit-up, scoot. Sit-up, scoot. He was getting closer and closer.

"Okay," yelled Ms. Strider at last. "Let's all go swim!"

We took off down the beach yelling and cheering. In the confusion of fifty-two fourth-graders jumping, diving, splashing, and causing general chaos, I lost track of Lawrence. As Henry and I caught up with Tom and Joe, we found out that they didn't know where King Kong's brother was either. They kept looking around them as if expecting to be clobbered any minute.

"Hey, this water's cold!" yelled Henry, splashing in.

"You have to keep moving to stay warm," advised Joe. He kept looking over his shoulder.

"I know," said Tom, glancing around him. "Let's swim out to the raft."

"Great idea," said Henry.

"Last one there is a rotten egg," I hollered as I pushed off in the direction of the raft.

It wasn't so very far from the shore. We were there and sitting on top of it in record time.

"Hey, look over there," said Henry, pointing to the beach. "There comes Dilly Duddle in his bathing suit."

"Oh, no...and look," I said. "Look who's running up to him with her brand new Wacky-Tacky Camera that her daddy bought her!"

"Ugh!" everyone groaned.

"Hey, let's play King-of-the-Mountain on this raft," suggested Joe.

"Great!" hollered Tom, as he pushed Joe off balance and right into the water. Joe caught Tom's leg and pulled him in. Before I knew what happened, Henry yelled, "Goodbye Bob!" and shoved me into the lake with the others.

"Come on, guys," said Tom, spitting the water out of his mouth. "Let's get that king off the mountain!"

"Yeah," we all agreed.

We were charging up the raft when I saw Lawrence struggling to get up the other side.

"It's Lawrence!"

As if by plan, the four of us dove into the lake all at the very same time and began to dash for safety. We didn't stop even when we reached the shore. We ran half-way up the beach before looking back.

"I don't see him," gasped Joe.

"Neither do I," panted Tom.

"You don't suppose he drowned?" I asked, coughing.

"No such luck!" said Henry, breathing hard.

Just then, one of the highlights of our great learning adventure took place. Something that we would talk about for days, weeks, and yes, even years to come.

It was right then that we heard Lawrence's booming voice, "I did it! I did it! Hey, everybody...I got 'em!"

Everyone on the beach and in the water turned to see what Lawrence was yelling about.

"Lookee! Lookee!" he yelled. "I got Joe's bathing suit. Lookee! Lookee!" He was prancing out of the water holding a bathing suit up high and laughing his head off.

"But..." I began, as we all looked at Joe. Even Joe looked to see if his suit was still there. It was, snugly wrapped around him.

"Joe...it's not yours," I said.

"But whose is it?" asked Tom.

All eyes searched for the owner of the missing suit.

"Oh, no!" screamed Henry. "Oh, no!" He was laughing so hard that he doubled over.

"Lawrence!" bellowed Ms. Strider. "Lawrence Lopp! You bring those bathing trunks here this minute. This minute, do you hear?"

"But Ms. Strider...Joe...he said my brother..."

"Lawrence Lopp...I don't want to hear one more word

out of you. *You* are in *big* trouble!"

"But Ms. Strider...it's just Joe... and he..."

"Not one more word, Lawrence...not one more. You hand me Mr. Duddle's bathing suit this instant!"

"Mr. Duddle!" Lawrence exclaimed.

By now, everyone was practically in hysterics. Everyone that is, except Ms. Strider, Lawrence, and, of course, Mr. Duddle. Mr. Duddle was angrily peering up over the side of the raft, shaking a fist in Lawrence's direction.

Chapter Four

"Welcome boys and girls...welcome to the Camp Crumb Talent Festival!" boomed Mr. Lowpitch's deep, melodic voice. We had all assembled around the blazing camp fire for the evening program activities. Most of us still had sore sides from laughing so hard at Mr. Duddle's misfortune. Lawrence, I might add, was very subdued after his colossal mistake and subsequent tongue-lashing from both Ms. Strider and Mr. Duddle. By now, he seemed to have forgotten all about the King Kong incident anyway. Lawrence's memory isn't the best even in good circumstances, let alone the state of shock he was in following the bathing trunks fiasco.

"Yes," continued Mr. Lowpitch, falling into the character of a TV show announcer, "tonight is special!... for it is..." he pulled out a small kazoo horn and tooted ta ta taaaaa, "the Camp Crumb Talent Festival!"

Everyone there was laughing and smiling at each other.

"Gosh," said Henry, "leave it to Mr. Lowpitch to think of bringing a horn."

"Yeah," I agreed, liking our music teacher more than ever.

"And to start off the festival, we are all going to learn to

sing the official Camp Crumb Song!" Saying this, he whipped out a baseball cap from his back pocket and jammed it on his head. Printed in big letters across the front of the cap was "Camp Crumb."

"Now...this song is easy to learn. E-A-S-Y." He glanced at Bernice. "You all know 'Take Me Out to the Ballgame' I'm sure." Everyone nodded in agreement. "Well, the official Camp Crumb Song has the same tune. It goes like this...

Take me out to that great camp,

Take me out to Camp Crumb,

Hiking and swimming and boating too,

Fun by the bushels is waiting for you,

So please take me out to that great camp,

Mrs. Tumtwit has it all planned,

For it's hip-hip-hooray we'll be there,

At that great Camp Crumb!"

"Yea!" everyone cheered Mr. Lowpitch's solo.

"Okay now, ladies and germs...oops...ladies and gentlemen," said our music teacher, still in character. "Let's hear it from the top. Alright...all together now...Take me out to that great camp."

After several more times through the official Camp Crumb Song, most everyone, except Lawrence, of course, knew it and was singing as loudly as possible with hands clapping out the rhythm.

"Okay...now that we're all warmed up and ready to go," said Mr. Lowpitch when we finished singing, "it's time to *prepare* for the great Camp Crumb Talent Festival. Yes...you heard me...I said PREPARE...not BEWARE! Whoa, you might say. Now just what does that wonderful teacher mean by *prepare?*" By now, of course, all of the campers were really enjoying themselves, including the adults. Mr. Lowpitch was talking fast and sounded like a barker at a carnival side-show.

"Well, I'll tell you right now that that *wonderful* teacher is *not* talking about a *pair* of anything! Oh no...no indeed not! He is, in fact, talking about getting ready. Getting ready for what, you may ask. Ha! Thought I couldn't answer that one, didn't you? Well...I can! What we have to get ready for is that fantastic...that one and only...never seen anywhere before...Camp Crumb Talent Festival!"

By this time there was so much laughter, we could hardly hear Mr. Lowpitch.

"Count off, I say!" he roared, turning his cap backwards and crouching down in a baseball catcher's position. "Count off by 10's. Here we go!" He pointed at Roberta to start us off. She was so startled that she just sat there with her mouth open, unable to say a thing.

"Not bad!" cried Mr. Lowpitch, "but I just bet we can do a little better than that!" We had all about collasped laughing.

"Okay now...we'll try it again. Roberta...listen closely. You begin by saying...are you ready...I know you can do it...begin by saying *one.*"

"One!" Roberta said loudly as she blushed.

"Fantastic!" praised Mr. Lowpitch. "Next?"

"Two!" yelled Cindy.

"Three!" followed Jane.

Each camper hollered out his number as Mr. Lowpitch went around the circle pointing from one to another.

"Now when I say the magic words," barked Mr. Lowpitch, "you will divide up into groups and...here it comes, folks...and PREPARE to do something for our Camp Crumb Talent Festival. It can be anything... anything at all! Just use your collective imaginations and come back to the circle ready to show your marvelous and original talent! And now...the magic words...Gravel Gray Grunt!"

I thought we would all pass out from laughing. I did notice that Mr. Duddle flinched when the magic words were said.

Within a few minutes the groups were busy preparing for our gala talent festival. I was a number five. So was Loretta. Two boys and girls from the other class rounded out our group.

"What will we do?" I asked, looking at the other group members.

"We can sing a song," suggested the other girl.

"That's a good idea," said Loretta.

We boys exchanged disgusted glances, and I said, "Oh, no. You're not going to get me to sing a song in front of the entire group."

"Me neither," added one of the boys. The other nodded in agreement.

"Do you have a better idea?" asked the girl.

I looked at the other boys. They both just shrugged.

"Good," said the girl. "We'll sing a song."

Within fifteen minutes all the campers had assembled around the camp fire. Mr. Lowpitch introduced group number one.

"Ladies and jerks...oops...gentlemen. It gives me great pain...oops, oops...great pleasure to introduce to you that fabulous group number one. I'm sure they will show you talent such as you have never seen before...and probably will never see again. Go to it, number one!"

Group number one was made up of two boys and two girls from the other class, with Bernice standing in the middle of them. She was beaming as though she was about to perform before the President of the United States. Without any hesitation they began to sing the official Camp Crumb Song. All except Bernice, that is. She just stood there smiling at the adoring fans.

"Why do you suppose Bernice isn't singing?" I whispered to Henry.

"They were practicing next to our group. She has a special part. She insisted. It's the 'hip-hip-hooray' part."

Group one was nearing Bernice's solo. "...and Mrs. Tumtwit has it all planned..." they sang. "For it's..."

Bernice stood there completely silent. No sound at all came from her lips. Not even a peep. The singers all looked at her. She just stood there, looking blankly back at them, oblivious to the fact that her part had come...and almost gone.

"Bernice," whispered one of the singers.

"What?" she whispered back. "What?"

"Hip-hip-hooray!" the singer prompted between gritted teeth.

It was as if a light bulb had gone on in Bernice's brain. She looked back at the audience and, without the least sign of embarrassment, sang loudly, "Hip-hip-hooray."

No one heard the finish of the song because of the almost hysterical laughter. Even Mr. Lowpitch was wiping his eyes.

All in all that evening, the campers were treated to the official Camp Crumb Song seven times. I have to confess that group five was one of the contributors. After hearing it sung for the seventh time, Mr. Lowpitch deadpanned that he was really almost dumbstruck by the originality shown in the talent festival. We all laughed along with him.

One of the groups showing some variation of ideas sang a different song. Another told riddles. The last group made a human pyramid.

Group four did the riddles, and it was a huge disaster. Most of them were simply stupid. For example, a kid named Todd asked, "What is round and can be eaten?" After incorrect guesses such as apples, pears, cherries, tomatoes, pumpkins and oranges, Lawrence guessed correctly...a banana! Don't ask me to explain...I can't!

Joe had the only good riddle in the group. He asked, "What is black and white and red all over?"

"A newspaper!" yelled Henry.

"That's right!" answered Joe.

"Ha, ha, ha...a newspaper!" laughed Lawrence. "Boy that's a good one. Ha, ha, ha! I never seen a red newspaper in my life! Ha, ha, ha! Boy...is that ever a dumb answer!"

Imagine that coming from the person who guessed a banana for something round that you can eat.

It was the last group, though, group ten...Lawrence's group...that really brought the house down! Their talent,

if you can call it that, was to make a human pyramid. Lawrence was chosen to be at center bottom purely on the basis of his sheer bulk. There was a boy on either side of him. They were all on their hands and knees. The two girls then got on their hands and knees on top of the boys. At last, the smallest kid, a boy, climbed up and *stood* on top of the girls' backs.

We all had just finished applauding when it happened. The boy took a careful bow and was about to climb down. Then disaster struck! There was a loud crackle in the fire. It was almost as loud as a gun going off! Well, evidently when this happened, a red hot spark shot out of the flames and landed right smack on Lawrence's behind!

"Yeow!" he screamed, and reared up like a bucking bronco.

"Look out!" cried one of the girls.

"What..." was all the boy on top could manage to say before tumbling down into the tangled heap that was once a human pyramid. That ended the talent festival.

Chapter Five

We all knew when the WUMP truck arrived. Music was blaring from its' speaker systems, and the driver was leaning on the horn. Everyone was waiting down at the beach to get sail-surfing instructions from Mr. Duddle. Oh yes, WUMP is Gravelsburg's own local radio station.

"Oh...it must be Mr. Rae!" exclaimed Mrs. Tumtwit. She rushed up the hill to greet *the* radio personality who concentrated his broadcasts on local happenings. Mr. Rae was rather new to WUMP. He took the place of Heather Heavenly when she left last fall. She interviewed people on her program called, "Goings On In Gravelsburg," until she accidently angered almost the entire listening population of WUMP. The station then freed her to return to her family owned butcher shop. Within a few weeks, Mr. Rae came along and was hired on the spot. He continued the interview style program, but preferred to travel around to different locations. He called his program, "Roving Round Gravelsburg with Rae." I personally thought that seventy miles was a little far to rove this time. But, as Mr. Duddle had told us, since this was the very first time an outdoor education program had ever been attempted in Gravelsburg, everyone was interested. WUMP could count on at least fifty-two families who would be tuned in for this particular program.

"Now then, boys and girls," began Mr. Duddle, glancing up the hill, "since this is our last afternoon at wonderful Camp Crumb, it's time for your lesson on sail-surfing. I personally will show you how it's done."

His whole manner seemed to have changed with the arrival of the WUMP truck.

"Over here...right this way," directed Mrs. Tumtwit. Following her down the hill was a smallish sort of man in a bright yellow suit. Behind him came a thin man in a T-shirt and blue jeans. He was staggering under a load of heavy equipment. "Boys and girls...I want you to greet Gravelsburg's very own celebrity, Mr. Rae. Let's show him how glad we are to see him here today!" shouted Mrs. Tumtwit.

A rather half-hearted cheer went up. None of us cared much for Mr. Rae or his program, but a lot of the adults in Gravelsburg listened to him.

"How *do* you *do*," he said dramatically, with a low, ground-sweeping bow.

"And, Mr. Rae, this is our principal, Mr. Duddle."

"Oh, hello there."

"Well, well...it's certainly nice meeting you Mr. Rae. My wife always listens to your 'Raving Rae' program." Then in a whisper, Mr. Duddle asked, "Are we on the air now?"

"The correct name of my program is 'Roving Round Gravelsburg with Rae,' and no...we're not on the air yet."

"Oh," seemed to be all Mr. Duddle could think of to say.

"Well, just go on about your business. My assistant and I have to set up our remote equipment." Mr. Rae waved the other man forward. "Salisbury...I will need the cordless mike for this show." He then turned back to Mr. Duddle and said, "You know...or maybe you don't...that this program is done live. There can be *no* retakes. Must be perfect the very first time!"

Mr. Duddle's face seemed to turn pale as he said, "Oh...of course...no problem...no problem at all. What do you want me to do?"

"Do? Why continue doing whatever it was that you were doing. You *were* doing something, weren't you?"

"We're on in two minutes, Mr. Rae," warned Salisbury.

Mr. Duddle looked as if he had been turned to stone. He neither moved nor spoke.

"Go on...go on. You were doing...what were you doing?"

"Lesson," croaked our principal.

"Lesson. Oh, wonderful, wonderful. A lesson that all these little kiddies' mommies and daddies can hear. Oh, it's simply simply super. Everyone listening will just love, love, love it!"

Now if Mr. Rae had spent a month trying to think of a way to insult us, he couldn't have done a better job of it. We looked at one another.

"Kiddies!" growled Joe.

"Mommies and daddies!" sputtered Tom.

"Does he think he's talking about kindergartners?" I asked.

Mr. Duddle seemed to have recovered his composure somewhat and was saying, "Now as I was beginning to explain...surf-sailing can be difficult for those inexperienced in sailing. I'll go slowly so everyone can understand my step-by-step procedure." He looked at Mr. Rae again and mouthed, "Are we on the air yet?"

"No, no...just go on."

"This is the surfboard...and that is the sail," Mr. Duddle pointed to the appropriate objects.

"You sure could have fooled me!" Tom whispered.

"Oh yeah," said Henry, "it's awful easy to get the two mixed up."

"Now, boys and girls..." Mr. Duddle was talking directly toward the mike Mr. Rae was holding with his back turned to us. "Do you see this pole? Good. This fits into the hole on the surfboard. You attach..."

"Thirty seconds till air time!" Salisbury hollered.

A flustered Mr. Duddle stammered, "...uh...uh...uh... you simply stick the sail into this hole."

"Mr. Duddle," called Tom.

"Yes, yes...what?"

"What do you do with the pole then?"

"Tom, you must pay attention. That's how accidents happen...people just don't listen. You place the pole in the hole of the surfboard, of course."

"But you just said to stick the sail there."

"No, no, no...wrong, Tom. We sometimes get mixed-up when we're nervous, you know. Now you musn't allow the

49

fact that we will all soon be on the radio make you so nervous. You must concentrate on what we're doing here. Be alert...don't be taken by surprise...that's rule number one for sail-surfing."

Salisbury began his loud countdown, "Three...two... one...Good afternoon, all you listeners out there in Gravelsburg. Welcome to today's 'Roving Round Gravelsburg with Rae' show. We have really 'roved' this time to bring you news of a new and exciting educational concept at our local elementary school. And now, direct from Camp Crumb is...Mr. Rae himself."

"Hello, hello, hello to each and every one of you. I hope that all my faithful listeners are just fine and dandy on this bee-utiful day."

Everyone, including Mr. Duddle, was dead silent, listening to the celebrity. He went on.

"Yes, today, we are indeed broadcasting...live...all the way from Camp Crumb. As most of you out in radioland know, Camp Crumb is the site for the first annual outdoor education experience for Gravelsburg Elementary School's fourth-graders. The principal has just begun a lesson for all the kiddies...let's listen in, shall we?"

"Uh...uh...yes...the sail...the sail for the sail-surfer..." Mr. Duddle's eyes seemed to be glued to Mr. Rae's mike. "This sail," he took a deep breath and began speaking very loudly and very slowly, "is tied to the pole. The pole fits into the surfboard."

"Mr. Duddle...Mr. Duddle!"

"Yes, Bernice?"

"My daddy's listening. I want to say 'hello' to him."

"No, not now, Bernice."

"HI DADDY!"

Mr. Rae *and* Mr. Duddle both glared at Bernice, but she didn't seem to notice. But then, she doesn't seem to notice much of anything anyway.

The radio celebrity resumed talking, "Yes folks, your very own Mr. Rae is now 'Roving' along the beach here at Camp Crumb...and what do you think he has found? Well...Mr. Rae has found this big group of kiddies sitting here listening to their dear Mr. Puddle teaching them about...about...some sort of sailboat."

"There he goes again," grumbled Joe.

"How does that there boat work?" asked Lawrence. He appeared to be fascinated by the sail-surfer and was totally ignoring everything else that was happening around him.

"Well, Lawrence...good question," Mr. Duddle had regained some of his composure. "I will demonstrate for you. You see, I was the captain of our sailing team in college. I was pretty good at sailing, if I do say so myself."

Lawrence interrupted, "But how does that there boat work?" he demanded.

Mr. Duddle forced a laugh. "Patience, Lawrence, my dear boy...patience. As I was saying, this sail-surfer is basically the same. As I've often said...sailing is sailing."

At the end of his speech, he turned and carried the sail surfer into the water. He didn't see Mr. Rae frantically motioning for him not to go out into the water.

"Well, well, folks..." said Mr. Rae, kicking off his shoes. "It looks as though dear Mr. Puddle is now *actually* going to demonstrate how to sail one of these contraptions." By then, he had one sock off and Salisbury

52

was helping him roll up his pant legs. "You folks at home are in for a real treat now. Roving Rae's going to follow this marvelous, marvelous school principal right into the water for his demonstration. Yes...right into the very cold water..." Mr. Rae's voice trailed off as his teeth began to chatter. He very carefully made his way into the lake to reach Mr. Duddle who had already placed the pole and sail onto the surfboard.

"Mr. Puddle," hollered Mr. Rae, "please tell us now what you are doing." He was now very close to the sailing expert and was stretching the mike out to him.

"Well...as you can see...I now have the boat and sail placed just so. I will now show how to make a perfect mount onto this narrow board. It takes excellent balance which I am proud to say I achieved while serving as sailing captain for Capful College."

"Oh, folks in radioland...how exciting this is," said Mr. Rae, snatching the mike away from Mr. Duddle. "Mr. Puddle is now placing his right foot squarely on the surfboard. His left hand is grasping the pole. Tell me, Mr. Puddle...why are you grasping the pole in this manner?"

Mr. Rae shoved the mike toward our principal. He answered, "I mount the sail surfboard in this manner to allow for maximum balance and sure-footedness. Any other mounting technique is certain to end with the board becoming unbalanced. This would make it capsize, you see."

"Oh ho...well, we wouldn't want that to happen, would we...not to all these little kiddies here." He turned back to Salisbury and mouthed, "How much more of this?" Salisbury held up three fingers, which I figured meant three more minutes.

"And now, Roving Rae listeners...our sailing expert is readying himself for the final assault. Yes...there he goes. Both feet are firmly placed on the board. Now he...oh, oh...something seems to be wrong...it's the sail...Mr. Puddle is having some difficulty with the sail. It's come loose and is flapping in the wind. Mr. Puddle...Mr. Puddle..."

Mr. Duddle paid no attention to the roving reporter for he was frantically attempting to keep his balance. The board lurched violently. Mr. Rae tried again.

"Mr. Puddle...what seems to be the problem?"

As he asked this, he stepped closer and shoved his mike right into Mr. Duddle's face. Just then, a gust of wind whipped the sail completely around both of them. Let me repeat that. *Both* the roving reporter and the expert sailor were enveloped in the sail! Over they went...right into the lake...mike and all!

Several campers screamed and shouted. Ms. Strider kicked off her sandals and surf dove into the lake.

Salisbury rushed up with another mike and half-yelled into it, "Ladies and gentlemen...please stand by! There's been a terrible accident...oh, just terrible...Mr. Rae and that other fellow...oh, no...they've disappeared under the water...oh, this is terrible...oh, I don't know if I can go on. Oh...but there goes the lifeguard...oh, she's disappeared too...what will we do? Oh, but look...there she is...and, yes...she has them...no. she doesn't...she has the sail...yes, yes there they are...oh, I'm not sure...oh, please, please!"

By now Salisbury was in a panic and sobbing into the

mike. "Oh, this is the most terrible thing...how could a tragedy like this have happened! But wait...wait. The lifeguard is unwrapping the sail. Oh, please let them be there...let them be alright! Yes, yes...she's lifting them both up! Oh, glory be! How wonderful! They seem to be unharmed."

By that time, all the campers were cheering and shouting as Salisbury rushed forward. He thrust the ever-present mike at Mr. Rae, "Please, Mr. Rae, tell your listeners that you're alright."

Mr. Rae paid no attention. He ignored Salisbury completely as he shouted at Mr. Duddle.

"You...you...you nincompoop! You idiot! You almost killed me! You've ruined my program! You've ruined my suit! Sailing expert! Why I wouldn't trust you with a wind-up toy boat in the bathtub!"

Having said that, Mr. Rae stalked off up the hill to the WUMP truck, leaving Salisbury standing next to Mr. Duddle.

Salisbury shifted from one foot to the other, then said, "Well, ladies and gentlemen, what an exciting program this has been. We seem to have about ten seconds. Perhaps I can get a comment from this ah...other man. Sir, would you like to make any closing statement?"

Mr. Duddle just groaned, pushed Salisbury out of his way and dripped back to his cabin, not looking behind him even once.

Epilogue

Our great learning adventure at Camp Crumb happened over two years ago, but I can still remember it vividly. So can most of the other kids who participated in this fantastic educational experiment. In fact, we had a contest for choosing a school mascot last year. You'll never guess what won out. Well...our school mascot is now, much to Mr. Duddle's embarrassment...a Gravel Gray Grunt!

Oh yes...Mr. Duddle did receive a full apology from both Mr. Rae and WUMP's manager. I suppose that helped him a little to endure all of the "expert sailor" jokes that traveled around town for the weeks following our camping excursion. Someone even put a sign on his front lawn that read, "Expert sailing instructions given here" with small letters at the bottom that read, "Suits washed while you wait."

There has never been another group from Gravelsburg Elementary School to participate in an outdoor education program since our visit to Camp Crumb. I figure that most likely there never will be, either.